P9-CBK-988

This book belongs to:

To my own Kùai, Vinson Ming-Da, with much love!
—Y.C.C.

In loving memory of Ya Wu and Jesse Lei.
—Y.X.

Immedium, Inc.
P.O. Box 31846
San Francisco, CA 94131
www.immedium.com

Text Copyright © 2016 Ying Chang Compestine
Illustrations Copyright © 2016 YongSheng Xuan

All rights reserved, including the right of reproduction in whole or in part in any form.
For information about special discounts for bulk purchases,
please contact Immedium Special Sales at sales@immedium.com.

First hardcover edition published 2001 by Holiday House.
First Immedium hardcover edition published 2016.

Book design by Joy Liu-Trujillo for Swash Design Studio
Chinese translation by Xiaoqing Chen and Carissa Duan

中文审校：白牛、邹海燕、张瀛

Printed in Malaysia
10 9 8 7 6 5 4 3 2 1

Library of Congress Cataloging-in-Publication Data

Compestine, Ying Chang.
The story of chopsticks / by Ying Chang Compestine ; illustrated by YongSheng Xuan. — 1st ed.
p. cm.
Summary: When Kùai cannot get enough to eat, he begins using sticks to grab foot too hot for the
hands, and soon all of China uses Kùai zi, or chopsticks.
ISBN: 0-8234-1526-0 (hardcover)
[1. Chopsticks—Fiction. 2. China—Fiction.]
I. Xuan, YongSheng, ill. II. Title: PZ7.C73615 St 2001
[E]—dc21
00-039615
ISBN: 978-1-59702-120-3

The Story of
Chopsticks

Amazing Chinese Inventions

筷子的故事
神奇的中国发明

By **Ying Chang Compestine** · 张瀛/文
Illustrated by **Yongsheng Xuan** · 宣永生/图

immedium

Immedium, Inc.   San Francisco

DiPietro Library
Franklin Pierce University
Rindge, NH 03461

Long ago, all Chinese people ate with their hands, including members of the Kang family.

The three Kang boys Pan, Ting, and especially the youngest, Kùai, loved to eat. Yet he never seemed to get enough food and was always hungry.

很久很久以前， 所有的中国人都是用手抓东西吃，康氏一家人也不例外。

康家的三个男孩，盼、廷、快都很能吃。尤其是最小的儿子快，他好像从来都吃不饱，总是觉得肚子饿。

One afternoon Mama called out, "Time to get ready for dinner! Papa, cut the chicken. Pan, peel the sweet potatoes. Ting, start the fire. Kùai, get water from the well."

Kùai's tummy rumbled as he breathed in the delicious smell. "If only I could eat my food right away," he thought. "But if I pick it up too soon, it burns my fingers. And if I wait too long, my brothers eat it all!"

"Let's eat! Boys, wash your hands!" shouted Mama.

一天下午，妈妈喊道："大家准备做晚饭啦！爸爸你负责杀鸡。<u>盼</u>，你削红薯皮。<u>廷</u>，你烧火。<u>快</u>，你去井里打水。"

很快，整个屋子弥漫着饭的香味，<u>快</u>的肚子开始咕咕叫了。他想："如果可以马上吃到饭就好了。

可是如果我马上抓起食物吃，会烫伤手。如果我等太久，哥哥们会把东西一扫而光。"

"吃饭啦！孩子们，先去洗手！"妈妈喊道。

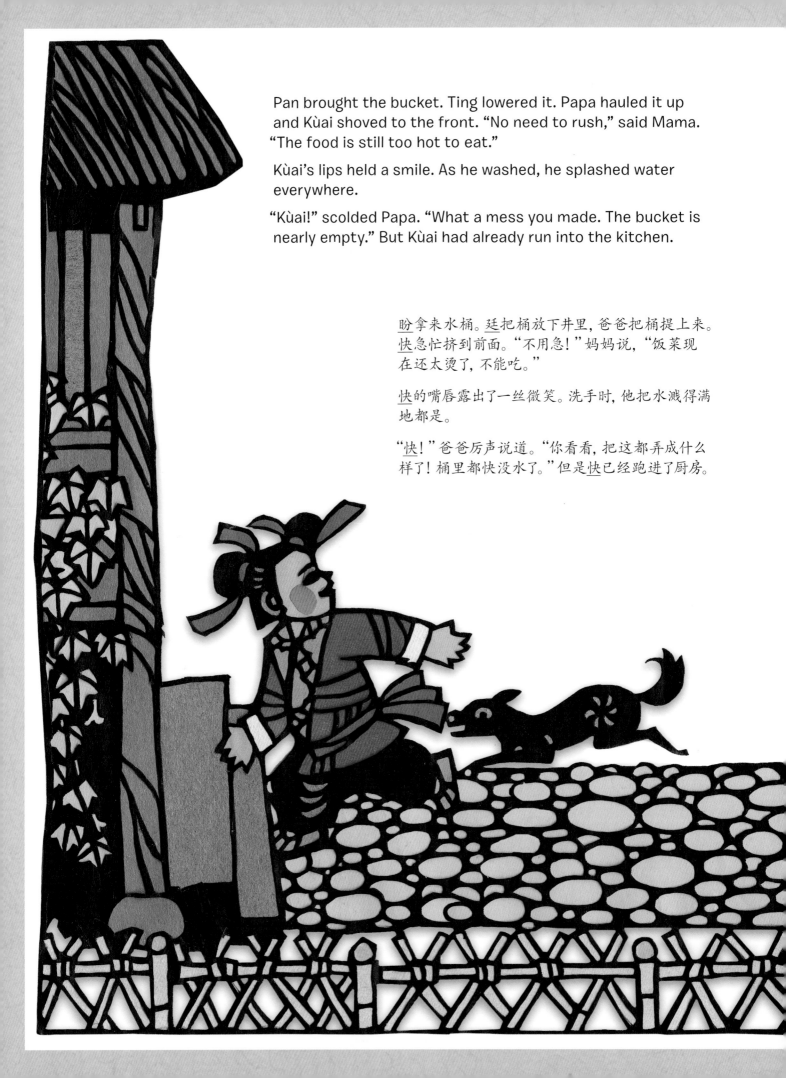

Pan brought the bucket. Ting lowered it. Papa hauled it up and Kùai shoved to the front. "No need to rush," said Mama. "The food is still too hot to eat."

Kùai's lips held a smile. As he washed, he splashed water everywhere.

"Kùai!" scolded Papa. "What a mess you made. The bucket is nearly empty." But Kùai had already run into the kitchen.

盼拿来水桶。廷把桶放下井里，爸爸把桶提上来。快急忙挤到前面。"不用急！"妈妈说，"饭菜现在还太烫了，不能吃。"

快的嘴唇露出了一丝微笑。洗手时，他把水溅得满地都是。

"快！"爸爸厉声说道。"你看看，把这都弄成什么样了！桶里都快没水了。"但是快已经跑进了厨房。

Papa sighed. "Could you help me, Ting?"

爸爸叹着气说:
"廷, 去帮我再打一桶水来。"

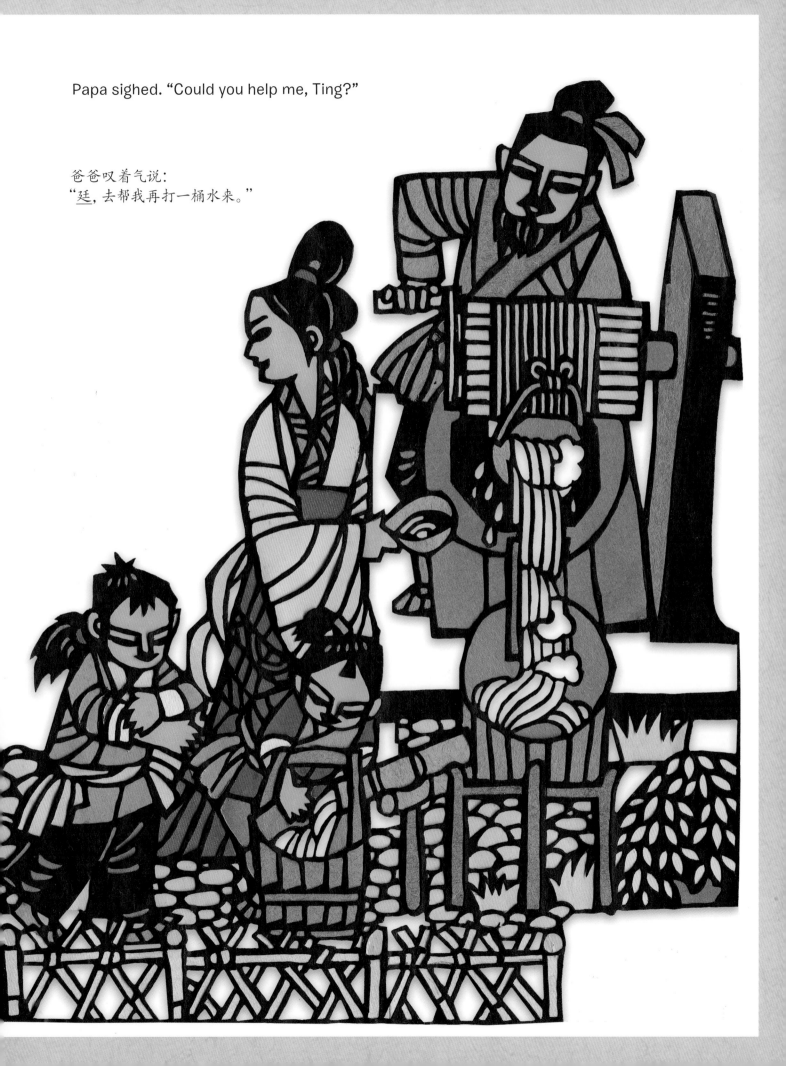

As Papa and Ting refilled the bucket, Kùai started his plan. He plucked two long twigs from the kindling by the stove. Then he speared a chicken leg with one stick and a big chunk of sweet potato with the other. He began to eat.

The hot food didn't burn his fingers. Better yet, he didn't have to race his brothers.

For once he was going to get enough to eat.

在爸爸和廷打水的时候, 快开始行动。他在炉边的柴火堆里抽出两根长树枝棍儿, 把一根戳进一只鸡腿, 另一根插进了一大块红薯。然后开始大吃起来。

虽然食物还是热烘烘的, 但是没有烫到快的手指。最让快满意的是, 他不用和他的两个哥哥抢东西吃了。

他终于可以吃个大饱。

When his family finally returned from the well, they were surprised. Ting understood immediately. He ran to the kindling and fetched two long twigs.

In a moment, Pan and Papa were climbing over each other, wrestling for twigs. "Ai yo!" they cried.

Kùai kept eating. Soon, everyone had a pair of twigs, even Mama.

当家人从井边回来时，他们都惊呆了。廷立刻明白了，他跑进厨房从柴火堆里找来两根树枝棍。

盼和爸爸也不甘落后，你争我夺地抢起树枝棍儿来。"哎哟，"他们大叫道。

快继续地吃。不一会儿，就连妈妈也拿了一对树枝棍。

"We should give these sticks a name," said Pan.

"Let's call them 'Kùai zi' to honor Kùai, the 'quick one' in our family," said Ting.

Kùai smiled. This was the first time that a family in China ate dinner with sticks instead of their hands.

"我们应该给这些树枝棍取个名字。"盼建议道。

"为了向我们家动作'快'的快表示敬意，我们就叫它 '筷子'吧。"廷说。

快笑了。这是中国家庭第一次用树枝棍儿代替手吃饭。

A few days later, Mama came home very excited. "Mr. Wang invited the whole village to his daughter's wedding. It will be a big banquet."

On the day of the wedding Papa carried a bundle of red silk, a symbol of celebration. Mama carried a basket of oranges, a symbol of wealth.

The boys secretly carried something too.

几天后, 妈妈回到家里, 非常兴奋地说: "王先生要给他女儿办一个盛大的婚宴。他邀请了村里所有的人。"

婚宴当天, 爸爸带上了一大捆贺喜用的红丝绸。妈妈带去了一篮子象征富贵的橘子。

三个孩子也秘密地带上了一些东西。

When they arrived, Kùai led his brothers to the table. "The food smells so good!" Ting grinned. "See the steam from that fish? It will be a long time before anyone can pick it up."

The children stared as the servants carried out dumplings, egg rolls, steamed buns, and sweet rice cakes. They inched closer, getting ready to strike.

Kùai whispered to his brothers, "Let's start!" The Kang boys whipped out their sticks and attacked the Butterfly Chicken, Wealthy Peony Beef, and especially the Sweet Eight Treasures Rice Pudding.

一到婚宴现场,快就把两个哥哥拉到餐桌边,说:"这饭菜真香啊!"廷咧嘴笑着说:"看那盘鱼上飘的热气吗?要等很久才可以吃呢。"

孩子们目不转睛地盯着仆人们端上饺子、蛋卷、包子还有甜年糕。他们又挪了挪身子,更加靠近餐桌,准备随时动手。

快对哥哥们小声说:"我们开始吧!"于是,康家孩子们快速地拿出他们的棍儿,对蝴蝶鸡块、富贵牛肉尤其是那八宝饭开始进攻。

The other children gaped. They tried to grab food with their hands but yelped, "Ai yo! It's too hot."

The smart ones ran to find their own sticks. Before long all the children followed. Some even climbed trees to break off the branches.

其他的孩子们都张大嘴巴吃惊地看着康家男孩们。他们用手去抓那些食物，但马上大叫道："哎哟! 烫死了。"

聪明些的孩子也跑出去找树枝。不多会儿，所有的孩子都跟着去了。有些甚至爬到树上去折树枝。

Suddenly, they heard a cry. "What is all this noise?" asked Mr. Wang. The grown-ups stopped eating.

Children returned with all kinds of sticks. A tall boy held two large branches. A toddler carried tiny twigs.

Papa opened his mouth, about to scold the boys, when Kùai put a big piece of meat in his mouth. "Try the chicken!" he cried. Now Papa was too busy chewing.

突然间，人们听到了一阵叫喊声。"这是什么声音？"王先生问道。大人们都放下了手中正在吃的东西。

孩子们拿着各式各样的树枝回来了。一个高个子男孩拿着两根大树枝。一个幼儿拿着一些细小的枝条。

康爸爸张开嘴正准备责骂他的孩子们，<u>快</u>将一大块肉塞进了他嘴里，说："尝尝这鸡肉！"康爸爸这时忙着嚼肉没有功夫去责骂他们了。

But Mama wasn't too busy. "Boys!" she cried, but Pan put a big piece of rice cake in her mouth.

Mr. Wang looked sternly at the children. "AI YO!" he cried. A hush fell over the crowd. Mr. Wang turned red. He began to shake. He was laughing!

Everyone else started to laugh too — even the bride and groom.

但康妈妈那时还没忙着吃东西。她大声喝道："儿子们！"盼马上把一大块年糕塞进了她嘴里。

王先生严肃地看着这些孩子们，叫道："哎哟！"大家都安静下来。王先生的脸憋得通红，身体开始颤抖。原来他是在笑。

在场的其他人也开始大笑——包括新娘新郎。

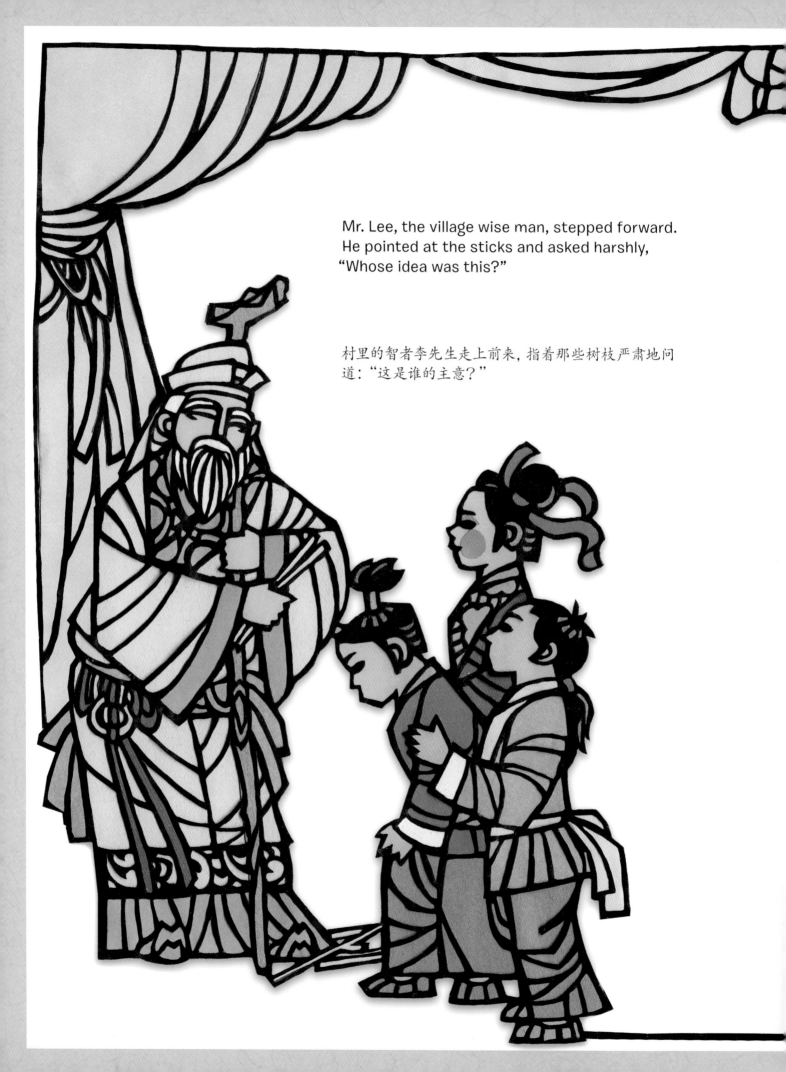

Mr. Lee, the village wise man, stepped forward. He pointed at the sticks and asked harshly, "Whose idea was this?"

村里的智者李先生走上前来，指着那些树枝严肃地问道："这是谁的主意？"

The Kang boys looked at one another. Ting stepped forward. "It was my idea. Please don't blame my brother."

Pan bowed respectfully to Mr. Lee. "No, it was my idea. Please don't blame my brother."

Before Kùai had a chance to say something, Papa walked over to Mr. Lee. "It is my fault, we did not teach our children manners. Please…"

Mr. Lee interrupted, "I must meet with the village leaders tomorrow morning. Your whole family shall attend."

康家男孩们互相交换眼色。廷走上前说:"这是我的主意。请不要责怪我的兄弟们。"

盼向李先生恭敬地鞠了一个躬,说:"不,这是我的主意,请不要责怪我的兄弟们。"

快还没来得及说些什么,康爸爸走向李先生,说:"这是我的错,李先生。我家教不严,请……"

李先生打断康爸爸的话说:"明早我要去与村里的长老们开会,你们全家都必须来。"

Early the next morning, Mr. Lee met with the scholar, the doctor, the matchmaker, and the Kang family.

He looked at the Kang boys. "Tell me who had the idea for the sticks." Kùai timidly raised his hand. "How did you come up with this idea?"

"I didn't want to wait for the food to cool," admitted Kùai. "I was always hungry because there was never enough food left for me."

第二天一大早，李先生与智者、村医、媒人，还有康氏一家人一起开会。

李先生看着康家男孩们，说："告诉我这拿树枝夹食物是谁的主意？"<u>快</u>怯生生地举起手来。"你是怎么想出这个主意的？"

<u>快</u>诚实地说："我不想等食物凉了再吃，而且剩下的总是不够我吃，所以我总是很饿。"

Mr. Lee frowned.
"Do these sticks have a name?"

"We call them 'Kùai zi' — quick ones," said Ting.

Mr. Lee turned to the other leaders. "I would like
your suggestions for the proper way to eat."

李先生皱着眉头，问道："这些树枝有名字吗？"

"我们叫它'筷子'—— 行动快的孩子。"廷答道。

李先生转向其他的长老们，说："我想听听你们的
意见。你们认为怎样用餐才对。"

The doctor said, "We should let our elders begin the meal."

"We should not stir food in serving bowls," said the matchmaker.

"We should cut food into bite size pieces," said the scholar. "What should we do about these Kùai zi?"

Mr. Lee smoothed his long white beard and sipped his tea. "None of these rules conflict with Kùai zi. I think using them is a good idea! I shall write a report and send it to the emperor."

村医说:"我们应该让长者先用餐。"

"我们不应该搅拌碗里的食物。" 媒人说道。

"食物应该切成小块。" 智者接着问:"我们应该怎样处理这些筷子呢?"

李先生捻着他长长的白胡子,喝了一口茶,说道:"这些规则并没有和使用筷子相矛盾。我觉得用筷子就餐是个好办法。我会给皇上写一份奏折禀告此事。"

Soon, even the emperor ate with Kùai zi. Before long, people were using them in every part of China.

From there the Kùai zi spread to other countries, including America, where they are called chopsticks, "quick sticks."

很快，皇上也用筷子用餐了。不久后，中国各地的人们都开始使用筷子。

筷子从中国传播到了其它国家，包括美国。在美国，筷子叫"chopsticks"。

As for the Kang family, they opened the very first chopstick factory. Their chopsticks, beautifully decorated with dragons, phoenixes, flowers, and luck letters, became famous.

Kùai was the happiest boy in China. His food was never too cold, and he always got enough to eat...

至于康氏一家，他们开办了第一家筷子工厂。他们的筷子名扬天下，上面绘有精美的龙、凤、花和幸运字母。

<u>快</u>也成为了全中国最开心的孩子。他吃的食物再也不会太凉，而且他总是能吃饱……

... sometimes even too much!

……有时甚至吃得太饱!

Author's Note

I got the idea for *The Story of Chopsticks* by watching my young son eat with his chopsticks.

Chopsticks originated in China, perhaps as early as the 11th century BCE. They are called "Kùai zi" (pronounced KHWY-*zzuh*) in Mandarin, which translates to "quick ones." In the pidgin English used by Chinese and European traders of old, "chop" meant "quick." Thus "quick sticks" became "chopsticks," which are frequently made of unadorned wood, bamboo, and plastic. Some are even intricately crafted from ivory, porcelain, or silver.

Confucianism, one of the dominant philosophies in China, strongly emphasized good manners. The Chinese were taught that it was bad manners to have a guest struggle cutting up their food. Instead, the host should cut the food in the kitchen. By substituting chopsticks for knives, the Chinese showed their respect for the scholar over the warrior.

Through the centuries the Chinese have developed several rules for eating with chopsticks:

- The meal should not start until the eldest person at the table raises his chopsticks.

- Chopsticks should not be set lengthwise cross the rice bowl. This symbolizes a coffin. Instead, they should be placed on a chopsticks stand to the right of the bowl, resting the tips on a stand.

- Chopsticks should not stand upright in a bowl of rice because it looks like a tombstone on a grave.

- Chopsticks should not be rattled against the bowl. It's believed this will break the wealth of future generations.

How to Use Chopsticks

1. Place one chopstick in the hollow between your thumb and index finger. Then rest the lower part of the stick on the tip of your ring finger.

2. Insert the second stick above the first one. Hold it the way you would hold a pencil.

3. Bring the tips of the two sticks together by moving the second stick with your index and middle fingers. The first chopstick should remain still.

Beginners can bind the sticks together at the top and hold them close the bottom.

Now you can use chopsticks to pick up food!

作者寄语

我是在儿子小时候看他用筷子吃饭时得到本书灵感的。

筷子起源于中国，最早可以追溯到公元前11世纪。筷子在普通话里读作"Kùaizi"，意思是"行动快的孩子"。那时中国和欧洲商人使用洋泾浜英文交流。其中"chop"是"快"(quick)的意思，因此"快的棍子"(quick sticks)变成了"chopsticks"。筷子通常是由不雕琢的木头、竹子和塑料做成。但是有些高档的筷子则是由象牙、瓷器或银子精雕细琢而成。

儒学是中国一大主流思想体系，它非常讲究礼数。中国人认为，让客人动手切盘里的食物不合乎礼数，而主人应该在厨房里将食物切好。同时，中国人用筷子而不用刀子进食，反映了中国有重文轻武的文化传统。

长期以来，中国人形成了一套使用筷子的礼仪与禁忌：

- 上桌吃饭时要请长者先动筷子。

- 不能将筷子横放在碗上，因为那样，筷子像棺材，所以筷子应放在饭碗右侧的搁架上。

- 不能将筷子直插在饭中间，因为那样，筷子像坟地的墓碑。

- 不能用筷子敲击碗盘，因为这样做被视为破坏后代的财运。

如何使用筷子

1. 将一根筷子的上端放在大拇指和食指的虎口处，无名指尖顶住筷子的下端。

2. 将另一根筷子放在第一根筷子上面，像握铅笔一样握住它。

3. 用食指和中指控制上面的筷子，将两根筷子尖部合起。夹食物时只动上面的那根筷子。

初学者可以将筷子上端用皮筋绑定，手指握住筷子下端。

然后就可以用筷子夹食物了！

Sweet Eight Treasures Rice Pudding

Makes 4 Servings   Preparation Time: 10 Minutes

Ingredients

1½ cups cooked warm sweet rice

½ cup chopped fresh mango

¼ cup raisins

¼ cup green candied cherries

¼ cup dried tart cherries

¼ cup chopped candied pineapple

½ cup almond butter

¼ cup maple syrup

Directions

1. Line the bottom of a 6- or 8-inch bowl with plastic wrap.
2. Decorate the bottom of the bowl with the mango and other fruit.
3. Pack half of the rice in the bowl in an even layer.
4. Spread the almond butter and syrup over the rice.
5. Cover with remaining rice.
6. Flatten firmly.
7. Invert onto a platter and serve warm.

八宝饭

四人份   准备时间: 10分钟

用料

1½ 杯煮好的温热糯米饭

½ 杯切碎的新鲜芒果

¼ 杯葡萄干

¼ 杯绿色的樱桃果脯

¼ 杯干红樱桃

¼ 杯切碎的菠萝果脯

½ 杯杏仁酱

¼ 杯的枫糖浆

做法

1. 在6或8英寸的碗里铺上塑料薄膜
2. 在碗的底部放入芒果和其它的水果做装饰
3. 将一半的糯米饭倒入碗中铺平
4. 将杏仁酱和枫糖浆均匀铺在糯米饭上
5. 将剩余的糯米饭倒入
6. 将糯米饭压紧
7. 将碗倒扣在盘上, 使八宝饭完全倒出摆盘, 温热食用